Threat to the Sea Otters

Elaine Pageler

High Noon Books
Novato, California

Cover Design: Jill Zwicky
Interior Illustrations: Tina Cash-Walsh

International Standard Book Number: 1-57128-005-7

0 9 8 7 6
3 2 1 0 9 8 7 6

Contents

Nate and Nell's mother is an ecology professor. During the year, Dr. Kidd teaches at a college. When summer comes, people invite her to meetings all around the country. Nate and Nell often travel with her.

"Ecology is man and nature living together in harmony," their mother always says.

Nate and Nell smile. "And we're the Kidds who help," they say.

CHAPTER 1

The Sea Otters

The ocean crashed in the distance. The twins, Nate and Nell Kidd, started down the path toward it. Both of them wore binoculars.

Their mother stayed in the cabin she had rented in Monterey, California. "Sorry I can't go with you. I must write my speech for the meeting tomorrow at the Sea Otter Rescue and Conservation Program. Look at the kelp beds. You might spot sea otters. But stay away from the water," Dr. Kidd called.

"O.K.," the twins shouted.

They rushed on. Ahead were some stairs. They took them down to the cove below.

Waves slammed against the sandy beach. Moist air from the spray landed on their faces. Nate licked his lips. They tasted salty.

"Look," Nell said. She pointed toward two boats out in the ocean.

The closest boat was just off the cove. A man sat in it with a fishing pole in his hands. The words "Jack's Tub" were painted on the side of the boat. Nell could read them without her binoculars.

The other boat was farther out in the ocean. It was a big fishing boat. Nell looked through her binoculars. "Watkins Fisheries," she read.

Now Nate was pointing off to one side. "There's the kelp beds floating in the water. But all I see are some logs," he said.

"Those aren't logs. They're sea otters. Let's climb these rocks. That will get us closer," Nell told him.

Nate followed her up the rocks and looked down at the water. "You're right," he said.

Three otters bobbed up and down in the kelp. They lay side by side on their backs. Two of them had their front paws straight up in the air. The third one had his paws folded over his eyes. All seemed to be wrapped up in the kelp.

"They're so cute," Nell said.

Three otters bobbed up and down in the kelp.

Nate laughed. "That kelp looks like seat belts around them," he said.

"Seat belts would be a good idea in this rough water," Nell told him.

Another otter was off to one side. She floated on her back, too. A baby rested on her stomach. The mother was busy licking its fur.

"How sweet," Nell said.

Nate pointed to another sea otter. "That one has something on her stomach, too. But it's not a baby. It looks more like a rock," he said.

As they watched, this otter pulled a clam from a pouch under her arm. She slammed it down on the rock. The clam shell popped open.

"That's smart," Nate said.

The otter lifted the clam up to her mouth. Just then there was a splash of water. An otter with a gray patch near one eye came up beside her. He grabbed the food from her paw and dived back into the water.

"Did you see that?" Nate asked.

Nell nodded. "There he is again," she said.

The otter swam toward the napping otters. He bumped each one on the head.

"What a pest!" Nell exclaimed.

Now the playful otter swam over to the mother. He turned flips around her and the baby. Water splashed all over them.

"You're right. Pest is a good name for him," Nate said.

Nell turned and spotted an artist up in the rocks behind them. "Let's climb up there and look at his painting," she said.

The painter seemed happy to show them his picture. "My name is Ward. I rented a cabin here so I could paint," he said.

Nell looked at the picture. "Aren't you going to paint in the boats?" she asked.

"Sure, that's next. Are you staying at the cabins, too?" Ward asked.

Nate nodded. "We better get back. Our mom is taking us to lunch," he said.

"I'll see you later," Ward told them.

The twins climbed down the rocks. They stopped to look at the sea otters again.

"Where's Pest?" Nell asked.

"Get out of here, you pest!" came a shout.

It came from the man in the small boat. He threw something at a gray-patched otter.

Nate laughed. "There's Pest," he said.

Dr. Kidd was still working on her speech when they got back. "Let's leave in an hour. When we return, we'll walk down to the cove."

It was one o'clock when they walked out to the car. Nate heard a sharp noise over the sound of the ocean. It seemed to come from the cove.

"That sounded like a gun shot," he said.

The Kidds waited but there were no other sounds. So they got in and drove to town.

CHAPTER 2

Trouble in the Cove

It was late when the Kidds got back from town. Nate's watch said 4:30 as they started down to the cove.

The tide was in now. Most of the sandy beach had disappeared. Big waves surrounded the rocks that Nate and Nell had stood on.

Nate needed his binoculars to see the kelp fields. "The three otters aren't sleeping any more. Instead they are cleaning themselves," he said.

"Otters spend a lot of time grooming. They must keep their fur coat clean or they will freeze," Dr. Kidd said.

"Whales live in the ocean. They don't freeze," Nate pointed out.

"Yes, but they have a layer of blubber. Otters only have their fur. Their coats may contain 8 million hairs. They trap air inside. It's important that the cold water never touch the otter's skin," his mother told him.

Suddenly they heard a screaming noise. It came from the direction of the otters.

"It's the baby. She's crying because she's alone. The mother has gone," Nell said.

"What can we do, Mom?" Nate asked.

"The mother has gone to get food. That's another thing that keeps the otters warm. They have huge appetites. A sea otter can eat 20 pounds of food a day," she told them.

There was a splash. The mother came up from the kelp with a clam. She rolled over on her back and pounded the clam on a rock. Then she lifted the baby to her chest and it stopped crying. Both of them started eating.

"Sea otters spend half of the day resting. One third is spent eating. The rest of their time they groom, swim, and play with other otters," Dr. Kidd explained.

"Playing with others reminds me of Pest. Where is he?" Nell asked.

Nate searched the kelp bed. Then he turned his binoculars to the other side of the cove. He saw something bobbing in the water.

"Maybe that's Pest. It looks like a sea otter," he said.

Dr. Kidd frowned. "Something is wrong with that otter. He's floating on his stomach. They always lie on their backs," she said.

"Will the tide wash him in?" Nate asked.

"I think so. Nell, go tell the manager to call for help. Explain that we have a dead or hurt sea otter here," Mom said.

Meanwhile Nate saw that there was some kelp wrapped around the otter. Maybe he could grab it and pull him in.

Mom picked up a board that had washed ashore. She and Nate waded out into the next big wave. Mom dropped the board behind the otter. Together they moved him onto the board and slowly back to shore.

"Pull the other side of the board. Let's get him to higher ground," Mom said.

Both of them tugged on the board. They dragged the otter to drier sand.

"Yes, that's Pest. See the gray patch near his eye. What's the red mark on the other side of his face? Nate asked.

Dr. Kidd bent over for a better look. "He's been shot," she said.

CHAPTER 3

Talking to the Sheriff

"What's going on?" called a voice.

Nate looked up. Ward was climbing down the high rock where he had been painting earlier.

"One of my brushes is lost. It could have dropped out of my painting bag. So I came down to look for it," Ward went on.

"Mom, this is Ward. He was in the cove when we were. He's an artist. You should see his beautiful painting. It looks just like this cove," Nate said.

Dr. Kidd shook Ward's hand. "So you were here earlier. Did you see the shooting?"

"What shooting?" Ward wanted to know.

"Someone shot a sea otter," Nate told him.

Ward's eyes widened and he shook his head. "No, I didn't see anything like that," he said.

Nell rushed down the steps. "Here comes the sheriff," she called.

Some men came down the steps behind her. The first one wore a star. He rushed over to the sea otter.

"Yes, this animal has been shot. He's lost a lot of blood but he may still be alive," the sheriff said.

"I hope so," Nate said.

Dr. Kidd nodded. "It looks like his head was caught up on the kelp. That kept him from drowning," she said.

"Quick, men! Get him in a net and take him to the Monterey Bay Aquarium. They have the best chance of saving him. I'll stay here and talk to these people," the sheriff told them.

Nate watched the men carry Pest away. Then he told the sheriff about being in the cove.

"The man in the small boat was really mad at Pest. He was throwing things at him when we left. That was about noon," Nell added.

"At one o'clock, my kids and I were getting into our car. We heard a sharp noise down here. It sounded like a gun shot," Mom said.

The sheriff turned to Ward. "What about you? When did you leave?" he asked.

"I finished my painting and went back to my cabin. That was shortly after the kids left. I was taking a nap by one o'clock. That must be why I didn't hear the shot," he said.

"Did you see anyone around the cove?" the sheriff asked.

Ward shook his head. "All I saw were these kids and two boats. Both boats were still here when I left," he said.

"The little boat was called Jack's Tub. The bigger one was some kind of Fisheries. I can't remember what. Maybe it started with a W," Nate told the sheriff.

"Ward painted the boats. His picture will tell us," Nell said.

"Yes, I did. But I didn't put a name on the big boat. It was too far away to see. I didn't have binoculars like you kids," he said.

"Was it Watkins Fisheries? That boat moors at the Monterey Wharf," the sheriff said.

"That's the name," Nate told him.

The sheriff turned to Dr. Kidd. "It looks like those fishermen are our prime suspects. Would you and your kids come along with me? I'd like to talk to those men," he said.

Nate didn't wait for Mom. "Sure we will. The man who shot Pest is evil. We want to help catch him," he said.

CHAPTER 4

The First Suspect

The sheriff started the car and headed toward the wharf. The road wound through the trees.

"Sea otters are so cute. Why would anyone want to shoot them?" Nell asked.

"Aren't they an endangered species?" Nate added.

"They are now. But once the entire Pacific coast from Alaska to Baja had plenty of sea otters. The worldwide population totaled 150,000 to 300,000," Dr. Kidd told them.

"That's a lot," Nell said.

Dr Kidd nodded. "California had 16,000 to 20,000 sea otters alone. Now there are only about 2,000." she said.

"What happened to them?" Nate asked.

"It was the fur trade. People wanted their beautiful coats. Hunters almost made the sea otters extinct in the 1700's and 1800's. By the early 1900's, only 1,000 to 2,000 otters were left on the entire Pacific coast. Just one small group survived south of Alaska. That was at Point Sur," Mom said.

"Isn't that near here?" Nell asked.

Dr. Kidd nodded. "Just a few miles south," she told her.

"How did they survive?" Nate asked.

"We don't know. A group of 32 otters were seen off Point Sur in 1915. Only a few people knew about them. They kept it a secret. The public didn't learn about the otters until 1938. That was after the coast highway was opened," Mom said.

By now, the sheriff was parking the car. Everyone got out and walked to the wharf.

The sheriff pointed ahead of them. "There's Jack's Tub now. It has just docked. The man is getting out with his fishing gear. Let's go talk to him," he said.

The man looked surprised when they walked up. "What do you want with me?" he asked.

"Are you the owner of that boat?" the sheriff asked.

"Yes, I am. My name is Jack Stone," the man told him.

The sheriff pointed to Nate and Nell. "These kids saw you fishing off Big Rock Cove. They say it was about noon. Is that right?" he asked.

"Sure, I was there. What's wrong with that?" Jack asked.

"Were you there at one o'clock?" the sheriff went on.

"No, I left at about 12:30 and went on to another place," Jack replied.

"Why did you leave?" the sheriff asked.

"Fishing wasn't good. There was a pesky otter that kept bothering me," Jack said.

"Did he have a gray patch near one eye?" Nate asked.

"Yes, that's the one. Say, what's all this about?" Jack demanded.

"That otter was shot at about one o'clock today," the sheriff told him.

A shocked look covered Jack's face. "It wasn't me. I'm a fisherman not a hunter. Go ahead and search my boat. There's no gun there," he said.

The sheriff did the search. "You're right. There is no gun. Did you see anyone near the cove when you left?" he asked.

A shocked look covered Jack's face.
"It wasn't me. I'm a fisherman not a hunter."

"I was busy running off the otter. So I didn't look at the beach. But there was one fishing boat further out in the ocean," Jack said.

"You may go. But give me your address," the sheriff told him.

Nate watched the man walk away. "Maybe Jack had a gun and hid it somewhere. He might have shot at the otter to scare him away. The bullet could have accidentally hit Pest," he said.

The sheriff took off his hat and rubbed his head. "Perhaps that's what happened. But I think we have a better suspect," he said.

CHAPTER 5

The Second Suspect

Nate glanced out to the bay. He pulled up his binoculars for a better look. "There's the Watkins Fisheries boat now," he said.

"Yes, that's the boat," Nell agreed.

"They'll dock in a few minutes. Let's sit here and wait for them," the sheriff said.

Mom thought that was a good idea. "Dinner will be late. I'll get some sodas," she said.

Nate turned to the sheriff. "Would those fishermen kill a sea otter?" he asked.

"Some of them might. Our fishermen don't like the otters much. Both the animals and the fisheries want the shellfish," the sheriff told him.

"You mean things like abalone and clams?" Nell asked.

"That's right. Otters love abalone and clams and other shellfish. The shellfish industries began in the 1900's. That's when otters were scarce. But now there are more of them. So the number of shellfish has grown smaller," the sheriff said.

Mom came back with the sodas and heard that. "It's not all the otters' fault. Some of the decline is due to overfishing," she said.

"That's true. The shellfish industries need better managing. Also, the otters help the kelp beds. They eat sea urchins who feed on kelp. People harvest kelp to get algin. It is used to make things like ice cream, toothpaste, and shaving cream. The California kelp industry makes about $50,000,000 a year," the sheriff told her.

"That's good. Then the sea otters are helpful after all," Nell said.

"Yes, they benefit us in other ways, too. They're lovable animals. Tourists come to our beaches to see them. They spend money when they come. This helps the economies of our towns," the sheriff told them.

By now the fishing boat had docked. A man was coming ashore. He wore a captain's hat. The other men still worked on the boat.

The sheriff walked over to him. "Are you the captain of this boat?" he asked.

"Sure, I'm Captain Mack. What's up?" the man asked.

"Your boat was seen off Big Rock Cove at noon. A sea otter was shot there about one o'clock. Do you know anything about it?" the sheriff asked.

Captain Mack shook his head. "Not a thing. We moved to another spot before one o'clock," he told them.

"Can you prove that?" the sheriff asked.

"Ask my men. They'll tell you the same thing," Captain Mack said.

The sheriff smiled at that. "Sure they will. But that's no alibi. Maybe you were using a gill net," he said.

Nate turned to his mother. "What's a gill net?" he asked.

"It's like a curtain placed between the ocean floor and the surface. Gill nets catch anything that comes along. Many sea otters have drowned in them," Dr. Kidd said.

The sheriff went on. "The otter swam toward your boat. You were afraid it would get caught in the net. Then your boat would get a fine. So you shot at the otter," he said.

Captain Mack shook his head. "I can't prove we moved on. No one was around. But we did. And we weren't using gill nets. You know the law. We can't get gill nets that close to shore now. My company doesn't want to pay a heavy fine," he said.

"May I come aboard and look around?" the sheriff asked.

Captain Mack didn't look happy about that. "I guess so," he mumbled.

Soon the sheriff came back and showed the Kidds a gun. "This was in the cabin. I'll test the bullets. But it looks as if we've caught the guilty ones," he said.

CHAPTER 6

A Surprise

The kids were back at their cabin later that night. They had just finished dinner.

Dr. Kidd was talking about sea otters again. "The fur trading was made illegal a long time ago. But still the sea otter is threatened," she told them.

"Is it because of the gill nets?" Nell asked.

"That's part of the problem. But laws are being passed to stop that, too. Sharks also kill otters," their mother said.

"So sharks eat sea otters," Nate said.

Mom shook her head. "No, they don't. Sharks are just curious. They snap at anything they see. Also, eagles eat a few."

"What about oil spills?" Nell asked.

"That's always a problem. The sea otters must keep their fur clean. A bad spill near here could endanger much of the California sea otter population. The U.S. Fish and Wildlife Services are trying to relocate some of the otters. But many swim back," Dr. Kidd said.

A knock sounded on the door. Nate rushed to open it.

There stood Ward. "I wanted to know what happened," he said.

Nate told him about Captain Mack. "The sheriff found a gun in his boat. He thinks the fishermen are guilty," he said.

"I'm glad they got caught. That otter was a cute fellow, and I hope he lives. Let me know if you hear anything more. I'm leaving in the morning," Ward said.

"We will," Nate told him.

The Kidds were tired. So they went to bed. The phone woke them the next morning.

Dr. Kidd took the call. She put down the phone and turned to Nate and Nell. "That was the sheriff. The gun doesn't match the bullet taken from Pest."

"The fishermen aren't guilty," Nate said.

Dr. Kidd nodded. "The sheriff wants to talk to you again. He'll be here about nine o'clock. We've overslept and I've got to hurry. My meeting is in an hour. The sheriff will drop you off at the Monterey Bay Aquarium. I'll pick you up later," she said.

Nate and Nell rushed around to help their mother. After Dr. Kidd drove away, Nate looked at the clock. It was 8:30.

"We have time to tell Ward. He wanted to know if anything happened," Nate said.

"Good idea," Nell agreed.

The twins rushed to Ward's cabin. The door was open. His things were still inside but he wasn't around.

"Maybe we can leave him a note. There must be a pencil and paper inside," Nate said.

It looked as if Ward was leaving soon. His suitcase, painting bag, picture, and a fishing net were all gathered together.

"There's a sheet of paper on the table. Hey, look at his picture. He never painted the boats. But he said he had. I wonder why?" Nell asked.

"I don't know why a painter has a fishing net either. But who cares? I need to find a pencil," Nate said.

He looked around. Maybe there was a pencil in Ward's painting bag. He started to open it.

Nell touched Ward's picture. "That's odd.

This paint is very thick. But it's completely dry. Ward just painted it yesterday. I thought it took oils longer to dry than that," she said.

Nate had the painting bag open now. It contained paints and brushes. They were very clean. Other thing were inside, too. Nate saw a beautiful piece of wood and some pipes.

His heart started pounding in his throat. "Nell, come here!" he gasped.

Nell looked into the bag. "What are those things?" she asked.

"Put them together and they make into a gun. I think we've found the guilty person," Nate told her.

CHAPTER 7

Good News for the Otters

Nell peeked out of the door. "I don't see Ward anywhere," she said.

Nate grabbed Ward's painting bag. "This is evidence. We'll take it to our cabin and wait for the sheriff," he said.

The twins ran down the path with the bag. They hurried into their cabin and locked the door.

Nate gave a sigh of relief. "We're safe now," he said.

"Ward didn't paint yesterday. He was just pretending," Nell said.

Nate nodded. "Ward waited until everyone was gone. Then he shot Pest. But the tide wouldn't wash the otter in for a few hours. So Ward took the painting and the bag to his cabin. Then he took his fish net down to the cove and waited," he said.

"Then Mom and you and I arrived We spoiled his plan," Nell added.

Nate searched through Ward's bag. He found a letter and read it. "There are laws to protect otters from fur hunters. But Ward gets rid of them in another country. This letter says he has sold several," he said.

"That's right! And you kids aren't going to stop me," a voice said.

Nate and Nell spun around. Ward stood in the bedroom door. He had a pistol in his hand.

"I saw you go into my cabin. You didn't come right out so you must have found something. I hid here to find out what it was. I'm glad I did. You have it all figured out," Ward said.

"You aren't a painter, are you?" Nell asked.

"No, I bought several paintings of places along the coast. I put the painting in front of me and hold a brush. Everyone thinks I'm an artist. I've made lots of money selling furs and I'll make more," Ward told them.

40

Ward stood in the bedroom door.
He had a pistol in his hand.

"Killing otters is horrible," Nell said.

Ward sneered and pointed to the door with his gun. "I like money better than sea otters. But you kids really enjoy them. So I'm giving you a chance to watch them for a long time," he said.

Nate didn't like the look on Ward's face. But they had to obey because Ward had a gun.

The twins started down the path. They heard Ward close behind. "Don't try running away," he warned them.

The tide was coming in. Big waves crashed at the bottom of the rocks. Soon the water would surround the rocks.

The sea otters were still in the kelp beds. They bobbed up and down in the water.

"Climb up on the rocks," Ward ordered.

"The tide is coming in," Nell protested.

Ward grinned. "That's right. You'll be safe if you stay on the top rocks. But the ocean will be all around you. It'll go down in a few hours. That will give me time to get away," he said.

"Stop where you are!" a voice shouted.

The twins whirled around. They saw the sheriff running toward them.

Nate's voice quivered when he talked. "Ward shot the sea otter," he said.

"I guessed that when I saw Ward with a gun. I got here in time to see the three of you going down the path," the sheriff said.

"That was lucky for us," Nell said.

43

"I've got more good news. Pest is going to live. No thanks to this guy here," the sheriff said as he clapped handcuffs on Ward.

Nearby three otters had been floating with rocks on their stomachs. Now they banged sea urchins against them.

"It sounds as if they're clapping. Maybe they're saying thank you," Nell said.

Nate laughed and clapped at them. "Thank you for eating sea urchins. We all help one another. That's what ecology is all about," he said.

"It's man and nature working together," Nell added.